Jan and Patch

Monica Hughes

Jan and Patch

Illustrations by Carlos Freire

FIRST NOVELS

The New Series

Formac Publishing Limited
Halifax, Nova Scotia

The development and pre-publication work on this project was
funded in part by the Canada/Nova Scotia Cooperation
Agreement on Cultural Development.

First publication in the United States, 1999

Formac Publishing Company Limited acknowledges the support
of the Canada Council and the Nova Scotia Department of
Education and Culture in the development of writing an
publishing in Canada.

Canadian Cataloguing in Publication Data

Hughes, Monica, 1925-

Jan and Patch

(First novels. The new series)

ISBN 0-88780-462-4 (pbk.) — ISBN 0-88780-463-2 (bound)

I. Freire, Carlos. II. Title. III. Series.

PS8565.U34J34 1998   jC813'.54   C98-950216-3

PZ7.H87364Ja 1998

Formac Publishing
Limited
5502 Atlantic Street
Halifax, NS B3H 1G4

Distributed in the U.S. by
Orca Book Publishers
P.O. Box 468   Custer, WA
U.S.A.   98240-0468   :

Printed and bound in Canada

Table of Contents

1
Full House

THE Beginning.

Did you ever long to have a puppy of your very own? Me too. I didn't mind not having one last year because Mrs. Thomas, who lived next door to us then, let me play with hers and take him for walks in the park. His name was Pete and he was so cute. I always kept him on the leash and took a plastic bag and a pooper scooper with us and watched carefully when crossing the road.

But now we've moved. Mom and I live with Gramma while

Dad looks for work up north. I sure do miss Pete.

"Please let me have a puppy," I beg Mom one day. "Just a little one. He'd be no trouble, I promise. I'd play with him and take him for walks."

"Jan, sweetie, I'm working all day and you're in school. That means Gramma would have to look after him."

That's all right, I think. *Gramma will love having a puppy. It'll keep her company when Mom and I are away, so she won't be lonely.*

"Gramma, I worry about you being lonely when I'm in school and Mom's at work," I tell her as we do the dinner dishes.

"Bless you, child, I'm never lonely. There's my exercise group

and my bridge club and my volunteer work in the hospital gift shop. Whatever made you think I might be lonely?"

"Oh, nothing." I put the big baking dish carefully on the table. *Maybe Gramma needs a guard dog*, I think.

"Do you ever get scared of burglars?" I ask as I dry the last glass.

"Gracious me, no! Why would I...? Jan MacDonald, what are you up to?" Gramma puts her hands on her hips and looks at me with blue eyes that are twinkly and stern at the same time.

"Nothing, Gramma."

"Nothing?"

"Well..." I feel my ears getting hot. "I was wondering if maybe you needed a dog," I say in a rush. "Just a little one. To keep you company and frighten burglars."

She shakes her head. "My little house is already as full as it can be with the three of us. I couldn't handle a puppy too." She looks at me over the top of her glasses. "Are you sure it isn't *you* who needs a dog?"

"Well, maybe. But he'd be yours too, Gramma. We could share him."

"I'm sorry, love, but NO."

Sometimes when grownups say 'no' you can change their minds for them, but the way Gramma said NO meant NO.

But I can't stop thinking about a puppy. I know exactly how he would look. White, with a fat pink tummy and a black patch on one ear. I'd call him Patch.

2
The Second Great Idea

I think about Patch before going to sleep, imagining him all warm and cosy on the bed next to my feet. I dream about him and the dream is so real that when I wake up I can almost feel he's there, snuggled against the small of my back.

Then the alarm goes off and Mom jumps out of bed and all the cold air rushes in. Just a dream. Life is so depressing!

"Hey, what's with you?" Sarah says on the way to school.

"Life is so depressing," I say.

"Couldn't do your arithmetic homework, huh?"

"No problem. It was a snap. But I need a puppy so badly."

"Why?" Sarah is always practical. She thinks I'm weird. But, though we are opposites, we're still best friends.

"Because..." I don't know how to put it into words. I know having a puppy has to do with moving to a new town, with going to a new school, with Dad being away. I try and explain this to Sarah.

"Like you're lonely?" she asks. "But you've got *me*. We're best friends."

"I know. But I can't cuddle you and have you sleep on the foot of my bed."

"Yuck! I should say not," Sarah laughs. We go into school.

In the middle of English class I get this great idea. *No problem.* I can hardly wait until recess to talk about it.

"Sarah, why don't *you* get a puppy and we can share it."

"Uh-huh." She shakes her head. "Horrible John will tease it. And anyway, I've got allergies."

John is her big brother. He took the heads off all her Barbie dolls and put bugs in her Pocket Pollies. Allergies I could argue about, but not big brothers. I sigh. "Life is so sad."

"Cheer up, Jan. I'll treat you to an ice-cream after school. I've got all my birthday money and there's a new Baskin-Robbins in the mall. You can pick your top favourite flavour."

3
Pet Store Pup

Sarah is a real friend. But even a double scoop of Rocky Road doesn't quite make up for not having a puppy. We walk through the mall imagining what we'd buy for all our friends and families if we won the lottery. I pick a new coat for Mom, and a waffle-maker for Gramma—I just love waffles. They're raffling a big red truck in the mall, so I pick that for Dad. And for Sarah, a TV set of her very own so she doesn't have to fight John over switching channels.

"Let's stop at the pet store. If you had a million dollars what would you buy there?"

"Why, I'd get a puppy..." I stop and throw the paper from my cone into the garbage. "What's the point? I'm not allowed anything."

"Cheer up, Jan. Let's go talk to Charlie."

Charlie is a green and yellow budgie that Sarah and I arc friends with. He belongs to the owner, Joanne, and she lets him out of his cage when the store's not busy. He's sitting on top of his cage when we go in. Right away he slides along the bars till he's close to us.

"Hullo, Charlie," Sarah says cheerfully.

He answers, "Charlie's a pretty bird," which is true.

"Hi, Charlie," I say, but I'm really thinking about puppies, not budgies. Charlie seems to know I'm sad. He flies onto my shoulder and starts nibbling at my ear. I can't help laughing. "Stop that, Charlie. It tickles."

"Why don't you ask your Mom if you can have a budgie?" Sarah suggests.

I shake my head, forgetting Charlie's on my shoulder. He flies back to the top of his cage and looks at me crossly. "You can't cuddle a bird. Not like a puppy."

As we go out of the store I notice a new cage by the entrance and then I see HIM. He's lying on his tummy with his

nose in his paws. He's white all over except for a black patch on one floppy ear. He's so still that his white hair blends into the white paper on the floor of his cage, and he's almost invisible.

I kneel down on the floor. "Oh, don't look so sad," I say. "It'll be okay. Somebody'll give you a nice home and love you."

I just wish it was me, I think.

He scrambles to his feet and pushes his nose into my hand. He's got a short fat tail that wags so hard his whole rear end wiggles. I can see the pink of his tummy through his hair.

"Oh, Patch, you're lovely," I whisper. He whines. It's like he is whispering back: *I love you too*.

"Come on," says Sarah. "Or we'll be late home."

I remember that I promised Gramma that I'd wash the salad greens for supper.

"Goodbye, Patch," I tell him. "I'll be back."

I look over my shoulder as we walk away. Patch is standing looking after me. He lets out a sad little yip.

"I'll think of *something*," I promise him.

4
Patch and Jan

Every day I go home by the mall after school so I can stop at the pet store and talk to Patch. He's always standing there with his tail wagging, waiting for me. Every day he gives an excited bark when he sees me. But when I leave it's a sad yip.

"I'll think of something," I promise him.

We talk to Charlie too.

Charlie says, "I'm a pretty bird." He nibbles my ear, but it isn't the same as when Patch pushes his nose into my hand and tells me how much he's missed me.

"Going to the mall all the time is getting boring," says Sarah one day. "Let's go home the other way by the park."

I know Patch will miss me if I don't go to the pet store, but I know I've got to be fair to Sarah. She just doesn't feel the way I do about Patch.

"Okay," I say. "Let's go." I try to look happy as we walk towards the park, even though I keep thinking that Patch is going to miss me.

Then I notice the kids playing with their dogs in the park, and grown-ups taking *their* dogs for walks. And I get this great idea.

"Wow! I knew I'd think of something!"

"What is it?" asks Sarah.

"I'm going to ask Joanne if I can take Patch for walks, the way I used to take Pete. I'm sure it would be good for him."

"Do you think she'd let you?" Sarah asks.

"Maybe if I *beg* her."

5
No Walks for Patch

Sarah's right, the way she usually is. Joanne shakes her head. "My dear, suppose something happened to him?"

"Nothing would. I *love* him."

She smiles. "I know. But I really *can't* let him out of the store."

I sigh. Charlie jumps onto my shoulder and nibbles my ear. "It's no good, Charlie," I tell him. "You can't cheer me up that way."

He doesn't listen. He walks around the back of my neck and pulls my hair. "Ouch, Charlie. That doesn't help at all."

When he gets tired of pulling my hair he flies over to Sarah, and I go to the front of the store and talk to Patch.

"You do need a walk, don't you?" I whisper. "I'd take great care crossing the road. I wouldn't let you off the leash. And I'd take a plastic bag and a pooper-scooper, so we'd leave the park clean."

Patch whines eagerly and his rear end waggles like mad. I look up at Joanne, the store owner, but she just smiles and shakes her head.

"Come on," Sarah reminds me. "We've got that project to finish for Mrs. Nelson."

Mrs. Nelson is our teacher, and she really likes us working together on art projects.

"I'll be back tomorrow, Patch," I promise. "I'll think of something."

Every day we visit the pet store and I ask Joanne, "Am I big enough to walk Patch yet?" She smiles and shakes her head. But I keep hoping. Mom measured me against the bathroom door and I'm taller than when we moved in with Gramma.

Mrs. Nelson asks us to write a story about a pet. I write about Patch, only I pretend he's really mine. I describe how warm he feels snuggled against my back just before I go to sleep. I get an 'A' from Mrs. Nelson.

"But it's not true," Sarah says practically.

"It might be," I tell her.

6
Charlie Takes Flight

The next day, when Sarah and I visit the pet shop, Joanne is in tears.

"Try not to worry." A woman with white hair is patting her hand. "He'll come back."

Joanne shakes her head and then blows her nose. "The mall is so big. He could be anywhere. And if he gets outside. . ." She mops her eyes again.

"Please, who's gone?" I ask.

Joanne blows her nose. "It's Charlie," she says. "He flew onto a customer's head and surprised her. So she jumped and hit out at him. He flew right out of the store. He'll never find his way back."

"Poor Charlie, he must be scared to death," I say. "But don't worry. Sarah and I'll look for him, won't we?"

"Sure," says Sarah, but as we go out the door she adds, "You're dreaming if you think we'll find him, Jan. The mall's huge and there are so many places where he could hide."

"I know, Sarah. But we've got to try."

We walk along the main mall, looking at the lights and the planters and the fountains. We look at the signs above the stores and under the benches where tired shoppers sit. We walk down the four cross-aisles

and back again. We search the food fair, under every table and chair. We ask all the people sitting there if they've seen a budgie. They all say no.

"I'm bushed," says Sarah. "Let's stop and get something to eat."

She buys some french fries and I get a doughnut with sprinkles. We take them out to the centre of the mall and sit down on the stone bench that runs around the big planter. It's full of palm trees and creepers, and spider plants like the ones Gramma has hanging in the living room.

"Boy, do my feet hurt," I say.

"Mine too. We're *never* going to find him."

"But we must. Think of poor Charlie. He must be scared to death."

I look at the noisy crowds around us, and imagine what it must be like to be a tiny bird. What would I do if I were Charlie? Where would I go?

I look up into the palms and the creepers hanging above my head. Is that a flower on that creeper? A *yellow* flower? I don't see any other flowers up there. I hardly dare breathe.

42

7
Rescue

"Sarah," I whisper. "Look. Am I imagining it?"

She follows my pointing finger. "It *is* him!"

I call out, "Charlie, pretty boy!" but there is so much noise, with the fountains and the music and everyone talking, he can't possibly hear me.

"What are we going to do, Sarah?"

"Maybe he's hungry as well as scared. You've still got a bite of doughnut left."

I break the remains of my dough-nut into crumbs and hold my

hand out. We look up into the creeper. Charlie doesn't move.

"Try whistling," Sarah suggests. "Joanne whistles to him."

I purse my lips and try to whistle. Nothing comes out. I hold my hand steady and wait. Sarah can't whistle either, but she makes a clicking noise with her tongue and I see Charlie shift his feet on his perch, the way he does when he's curious.

"Do it again," I whisper.

She does. I can see Charlie's head tilt and his beady black eye looking down at us. Then, suddenly, he is sitting on my hand, pecking at the crumbs. Quickly I cup my other hand over his body. I can feel him shiver and flutter. I hold him softly.

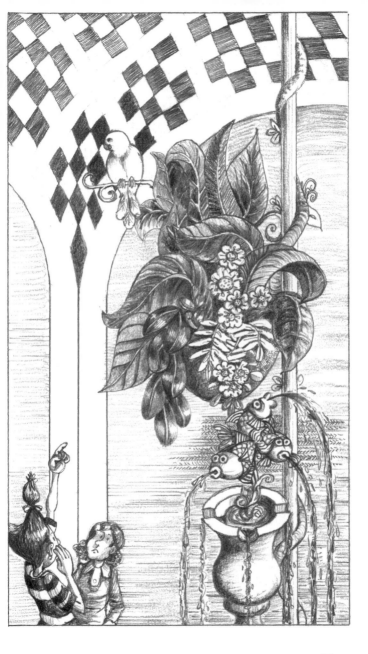

45

"It's okay, Charlie," I whisper against my closed hands. "We'll take you safe home."

Joanne is so pleased to see Charlie that she cries all over again. She puts him safely in his cage, and then we have to run, because we're really late home.

8
Shopping with Gramma

Next day is Saturday, and Sarah has piano lessons. Gramma and I go to the mall, and I introduce her to Patch.

"Oh, he *is* sweet," she says. Just for a minute I think she's going to relent and let us take Patch home. But she catches me watching her, and she shakes her head and moves on. "Come on, Jan. We're getting late and I want to look at those tea towels."

Joanne runs after us. "My dear, you never gave me a chance to thank you for saving Charlie.

You were so clever and resourceful. I would like to give you and
your friend a small reward."

I find my ears are getting red.
Gramma is looking astonished.

"It's all right," I tell Joanne.
"Charlie's our friend too."

"I must do *something*," says
Joanne.

"It's all right, really," I say
again. "We did it for Charlie."

"What was *that* all about?"
Gramma asks, as Joanne runs
back to the pet shop. "Who's
Charlie and how did you save
his life?"

I have to explain.

"How very resourceful of you,"
she says.

Resourceful. Hmm. As we finish Gramma's shopping I get
another great idea.

50

9
The Best Reward of All

Next day, on the way to school, I tell Sarah about my great idea. "Don't you think I'm resourceful enough and big enough to take Patch for walks?" I ask her.

Sarah shrugs. "I guess so. But if Joanne wants to be grateful and reward us, I'd sooner have a couple of loonies."

"Oh, Sarah, how can a loonie match up to *Patch*?"

She sighs. "Okay, then. Let's go talk to Joanne after school."

"You're a real friend."

"I know I am, Jan. And you're a real nut."

So after school we go the pet shop. Joanne gives us a big smile. "I hope you've changed your mind about letting me reward you for saving Charlie," she says. She opens the cash drawer.

I can hear Sarah give a heavy sigh beside me.

"Yes, please," I say quickly. "I thought maybe you'd see we were truly resourceful and old enough now to take Patch for walks."

Joanne looks from me to Sarah and then down at Patch, who is standing on his hind legs, whining to be let out. She closes the cash drawer and smiles.

"Well..." she says slowly. And I know I've won.

Now every day after school Sarah and I take Patch on his

leash over to the park. *I* carry the bag and the pooper scooper. That's the bargain I had to make with Sarah. But she loves him too, and outdoors her allergies aren't a problem.

Sometimes she likes to bug me. "I wonder what sort of reward Joanne had in mind? What would I have bought with it?"

"It couldn't possibly be as nice as taking Patch for a run, could it?"

"I guess not. But you know what, Jan? One day someone's going to buy Patch. What'll you do then?"

I wish Sarah wasn't so practical. But Patch does need a real home, I know that.

Then I think, *maybe Dad will come south soon, and we'll have a house of our own and a puppy of our own, who'll snuggle on my bed at nights.*

The more I think about this the more real it becomes. One day it'll happen. I know it will!

THE END

THE END

56

About the Author...

MONICA HUGHES lives in Edmonton, Alberta. She is the author of 28 books including *Jan and Patch* as well as *Jan's Big Bang*. A few of her many awards include the Vicky Metcalf Award, the Writers Guild of Alberta Award and the Canada Council Prize for Children's Literature.

About the Illustrator...

CARLOS FREIRE lives in Toronto. He is an illustrator who apprenticed with a leading muralist in his native Chile. He has illustrated *Jan and Patch* as well as *Jan's Big Bang* and numerous books that have been published throughout the world.

58

Another story about Jan...

• *Jan's Big Bang*
by Monica Hughes/Illustrated by Carlos Freire
Taking part in the Science Fair is a big deal for Grade 3 kids, but Jan and her best friend Sarah are ready for the challenge. Still, finding a safe project isn't easy, and the girls discover that getting ready for the fair can cause a whole lot of trouble.

Meet five other great kids in the New First Novels Series...

Meet Morgan in

• *Morgan and the Money*
by Ted Staunton/Illustrated by Bill Slavin
When money for the class trip goes missing, Morgan wonders who to tell about seeing Aldeen Hummel, the Godzilla of Grade 3, at the teacher's desk with the envelope. Morgan only wants to do the right thing, but it's hard to know if not telling all the truth would be the same as telling a lie.

• *Morgan Makes Magic*

by Ted Staunton/Illustrated by Bill Slavin

When he's in a tight spot, Morgan tells stories — and most of them stretch the truth, to say the least. But when he tells kids at his new school he can do magic tricks, he really gets in trouble — most of all with the dreaded Aldeen Hummel!

Meet Lilly in

• *Lilly's Good Deed*

by Brenda Bellingham/Illustrated by Kathy Kaulbach

Lilly can't stand Theresa Green. Now she is living on Lilly's street and making trouble. First, Lilly's friend Minna gets hurt because of Theresa's clumsiness, then Lilly is hurled off her bike when Theresa gets in the way. But when they have to work together to save the life of a kitten, Lilly has a change of heart.

• *Lilly to the Rescue*

by Brenda Bellingham/Illustrated by Kathy Kaulbach

Bossy-boots! That's what kids at school start calling Lilly when she gives a lot of advice that's not wanted. Lilly can't help telling people what to do — but how can she keep any of her friends if she always knows better?

Meet Robyn in

• *Robyn's Want Ad*

by Hazel Hutchins/Illustrated by
Yvonne Cathcart

Robyn is fed up with being an only child. She decides that having a part-time brother would be ideal. But the only person who answers her classified ad is her neighbour Ari and he wants Robyn to teach him piano. All she wanted was a brother, plain and simple, and now she's mixed up in Ari's plot to avoid his real piano lessons.

• *Shoot for the Moon, Robyn*

by Hazel Hutchins/Illustrated by
Yvonne Cathcart

When the teacher asks her to sing for the class, Robyn knows it's her chance to be the world's best singer. Should she perform like Celine Dion, or do *My Bonnie Lies Over the Ocean*, or the matchmaker song? It's hard to decide, even for the world's best singer — and the three boys who throw spitballs don't make it any easier.

Meet Carrie in

• *Carrie's Crowd*

by Lesley Choyce/Illustrated by Mark Thurman
Carrie wants to be part of the cool crowd.
Becoming friends with them means getting
a new image for herself but it also means
ignoring her old friends. That's when
Carrie starts to see that there are
friends, and then there are good friends.

• *Go For It, Carrie*

by Lesley Choyce/Illustrated by Mark Thurman
More than anything else, Carrie wants to
roller-blade. Her big brother and his friend
just laugh at her. But Carrie knows she can
do it if she just keeps trying. As her friend
Gregory tells her, "You can do it, Carrie. Go
for it!"

Meet Duff in

• *Duff the Giant Killer*

by Budge Wilson/Illustrated by Kim LaFave
Getting over the chicken pox can be boring,
but Duff and Simon find a great way to
enjoy themselves — acting out one of
their favourite stories, *Jack the Giant Killer*,
in the park. In fact, they do it so well the
police get into the act.

Look for these First Novels!

• *About Arthur*
Arthur Throws a Tantrum
Arthur's Dad
Arthur's Problem Puppy

• *About Fred*
Fred and the Flood
Fred and the Stinky Cheese
Fred's Dream Cat

• *About the Loonies*
Loonie Summer
The Loonies Arrive

• *About Maddie*
Maddie in Trouble
Maddie in Hospital
Maddie Goes to Paris
Maddie in Danger
Maddie in Goal
Maddie Wants Music
That's Enough Maddie!

• *About Mikey*
Mikey Mite's Best Present
Good For You, Mikey Mite!
Mikey Mite Goes to School
Mikey Mite's Big Problem

• *About Mooch*
Mooch Forever
Hang On, Mooch!
Mooch Gets Jealous
Mooch and Me

• *About the Swank Twins*
The Swank Prank
Swank Talk

• *About Max*
Max the Superhero

• *About Will*
Will and His World

Formac Publishing Company Limited
5502 Atlantic Street, Halifax, Nova Scotia B3H 1G4
Orders: 1-800-565-1975 Fax: (902) 425-0166